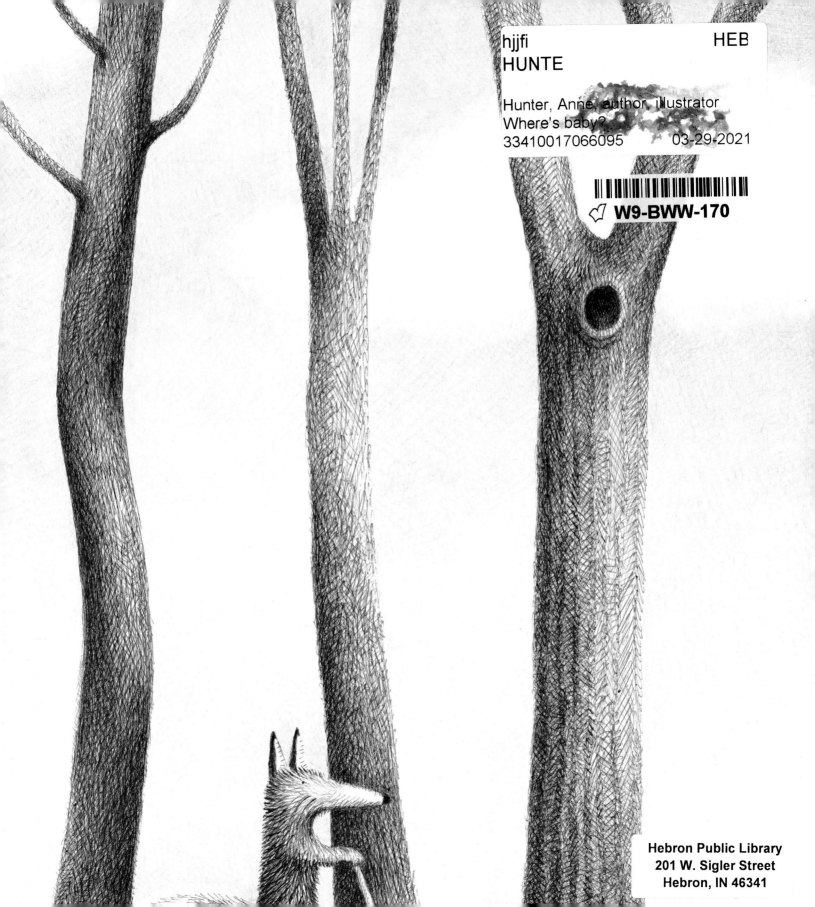

Tundra Books, an imprint of Penguin Random House Canada Young Readers,
a Penguin Random House Company

Library and Archives Canada Cataloguing in Publication
Title: Where's baby? / by Anne Hunter.
Other titles: Where is baby?
Names: Hunter, Anne, author, illustrator.
Identifiers: Canadiana (print) 20190054506 | Canadiana (ebook) 20190054522 |
ISBN 9780735264984 (hardcover) | ISBN 9780735264991 (EPUB)
Subjects: LCSH: English language–Prepositions–Juvenile literature. | LCSH: Hide-and-seek–Juvenile literature.
Classification: LCC PE1335 .H86 2020 | DDC j425.7–dc23

Published simultaneously in the United States of America by Tundra Books of Northern New York,
an imprint of Penguin Random House Canada Young Readers, a Penguin Random House Company

Library of Congress Control Number: 2019930343

Edited by Samantha Swenson
Designed by John Martz
The artwork in this book was rendered in ballpoint pen and colored pencil.
The text was hand lettered by Anne Hunter.

Printed and bound in China

www.penguinrandomhouse.ca

1 2 3 4 5   24 23 22 21 20

Anne Hunter

Where's Baby?

tundra